This book belongs to

Kaily Kaily

Mohn

Buried Treasure!

Tales from Bikini Bottom

Stephen Hillenburg

Based on the TV series *SpongeBob SquarePants*® created by Stephen Hillenburg as seen on Nickelodeon®

SIMON SPOTLIGHT

An imprint of Simon & Schuster Children's Publishing Division

1230 Avenue of the Americas, New York, New York 10020

Manufactured in the United States of America

First Edition

2 4 6 8 10 9 7 5 3 1

ISBN 0-689-87467-7

These titles were previously published individually by Simon Spotlight.

Buried Treasure!
Tales from Bikini Bottom

Simon Spotlight/Nickelodeon

New York   London   Toronto   Sydney

TABLE OF CONTENTS

And the Winner Is . . .

89 paces

SpongeBob and the Princess

115 paces

Bottoms Up! Jokes from Bikini Bottom

141 paces

The Amazing SpongeBobini

by Steven Banks

illustrated by Heather Martinez

"Patrick, look!" shouted SpongeBob. "The Stingray Brothers & Barnacle Bay Shrimp's Circus is coming! The greatest show under the sea!"

"Too bad we don't live under the sea," said Patrick. "I wish the circus would come to Bikini Bottom."

"Patrick, Bikini Bottom *is* under the sea!" SpongeBob said.

"Oh," said Patrick, scratching his head, "I always wondered why there were so many fish around here."

The Stingray Brothers & Barnacle Bay Shrimp's Circus

The Greatest Show Under the Sea!

The next day SpongeBob knocked on Patrick's rock. "Patrick, it's circus time! We'd better leave now so we can get seats by the jugglers and clowns. Real, live clowns, Patrick! Let's go!"

There was no answer. He knocked again. "Patrick?" called SpongeBob.

SpongeBob lifted the rock and saw Patrick lying in bed. "Patrick, what are you doing in bed?" he asked. "We're going to the circus!"

Patrick shook his head sadly. "I can't go to the circus, SpongeBob. I'm sick!"

"Don't worry," said SpongeBob. "I know how to make you feel better. I'll sing you the 'Get Well' song. My grandma used to sing it to me when I was sick."

SpongeBob cleared his throat and began to sing:

"Get well, Patrick. Don't be sick!
This little song will do the trick!
La, la, la—you'll feel better,
by the time I knit this sweater!"

The song didn't work. Patrick was still sick.
"I know—I'll do the 'Get Well' dance!" said SpongeBob.
He began to jump around Patrick's bed. But that didn't work either.

Next SpongeBob tried hypnotizing Patrick.
"Look deep into my eyes and listen to my soothing voice. You are not sick, Patrick. You will go to the circus with your best friend, SpongeBob."

"AH-CHOO!" Patrick sneezed.

SpongeBob patted Pat's head, "Well, we gave it the old boating-school try. . . . See you later, Patrick. I'm off to the most fabulous, amazing, colossal circus ever!"

Patrick grabbed SpongeBob. "But you've got to stay here!" he pleaded. "You have to get sick too! Then we can be sick together and miss the circus together and not have any fun together!"

"Uh, that sounds great, Patrick," said SpongeBob. "But I'm not sick and I really, really, really want to see the circus!"

"Fine!" said Patrick. "Go! I'll just be sick and miss the circus and not have fun all by myself!"

"Great! I knew you'd understand," SpongeBob called over his shoulder. "I'll bring you some of those circus peanuts you love so much!"

SpongeBob gazed up at the huge, red circus tent. "So *that's* why they call it the big top," he said as he handed over his ticket.

SpongeBob hurried to his seat right next to the ring.
"Ladies and gentlemen!" called the ringmaster.
"Welcome to the greatest show under the sea!"

It *was* the greatest show under the sea. There were acrobats and jugglers, trapeze artists and tightrope walkers, and they even shot a fish out of a cannon! SpongeBob was eating popcorn and watching the show.

"Wow!" cried SpongeBob, "Isn't this the greatest show you've ever seen, Patrick?" He turned and looked at the empty seat beside him. SpongeBob had forgotten that Patrick wasn't there.

Everyone was laughing at the clowns except for SpongeBob. He couldn't stop thinking about Patrick. He started to cry. "I can't enjoy the circus while my best friend is home sick! Patrick needs me. I must return to his bedside and do what any self-respecting sponge would do for a friend in need!"

Patrick was asleep in bed when suddenly he heard a voice outside that woke him up.

"Ladies and gentlemen and all starfish named Patrick!" yelled the voice.

My name is Patrick, thought Patrick. And I'm a starfish!

He got out of bed and lifted up his rock and he couldn't believe what he saw. . . .

SpongeBob was wearing a top hat and a fake mustache. "Welcome to the second greatest show under the sea, SpongeBob's Almost-as-Good-as-a-Real-Circus Circus!" he announced.

Patrick jumped up and down excitedly. "Where is the circus? Where is it? Where?"

"It's *me!*" said SpongeBob. "*I'm* the circus!"

Patrick looked puzzled. "But you don't look like a circus. You look like SpongeBob."

"Just watch!" said SpongeBob.

"Our first act will be SpongeBobini the amazing juggler!" said SpongeBob. "I will attempt to balance ten Krabby Patties on my head while juggling five spatulas!"

"And now prepare yourselves for the death-defying tightrope walk of terror!" he continued.

Patrick hid under his pillow. "That sounds scary! Tell me when it's over! I can't look!"

"And now the Amazing SpongeBobini will swallow a clarinet!"
said SpongeBob. "Don't try this at home, kids!"
"Too late," mumbled Patrick.

SpongeBob performed all
the different acts he had seen
at the circus.

"And now for the grand finale—a brave, handsome soul will be shot out of a cannon!" announced SpongeBob.

"Be careful brave, handsome soul!" shouted Patrick.

SpongeBob took a final bow, exhausted.

Patrick clapped and cheered. "That was a great circus, SpongeBob! I wish you could have been there to see it! Now you sit down and I'll show you what you missed."

SpongeBob smiled. "Wait a minute. Aren't you sick?" he asked.

"Not anymore!" shouted Patrick. "The circus cured me!"

Hands OFF!

by David Lewman

illustrated by C. H. Greenblatt and William Reiss

SpongeBob was playing with his best friend, Patrick. He slid down Patrick's rock, sprinted over to Squidward's house, and ran up the side.

"Beat that!" yelled SpongeBob happily. "That's my fastest time yet!"

"Oh, yeah?" shouted Patrick. "I bet I can do it even slower! I mean—faster!"

Squidward leaned out of his window. "Will you two be quiet?!" he said, snarling. "I'm trying to practice my clarinet!"

"But, Squidward, we're playing a really fun game," Patrick explained. "See, you slide down my rock, then you zip over to your house, and run up the side—"

"I *know* what you're doing," said Squidward, interrupting. "Just stop it! You're being too loud!"

"Why don't you play with us, Squidward?" asked SpongeBob. "It's fun!"

Squidward noticed the mailman pulling up to SpongeBob's house.

"Why look, SpongeBob," he said, pointing. "Isn't that the mailman at your house? It looks like he's carrying a box. . . ."

"A box!" shouted SpongeBob. "That's just what I've been waiting for!"

To:
SpongeBob
SquarePants

This Side Up

MAIL

SpongeBob carefully opened the box. "At last," he whispered. "Do you realize what this is, Patrick?"

Patrick nodded. "I have no idea," he said slowly.

SpongeBob trembled with excitement. "This," he explained, "is a genuine Mermaid Man and Barnacle Boy Bubble Blower . . . in its original packaging!"

Command the Creatures of the Deep!

MERMAID MAN AND BARNACLE BOY

BUBBLE

Made in the China Sea

"Wow," said Patrick. "What does that mean?"

SpongeBob gently lifted the Bubble Blower and stared at it. "I've been trying to find one of these for years. Isn't it great?"

Patrick jumped up and down with excitement. "I love Mermaid Man and Barnacle Boy! Come on, SpongeBob—let's blow some bubbles! I'll bet they'll be the best bubbles in the whole world!"

SpongeBob looked shocked. "Blow some bubbles? But, Patrick, we can't open this. We have to leave it in the original packaging."

Patrick scratched his head. "Why? What good is a toy if you can't play with it?"

SpongeBob smiled. "Oh, Patrick," he said. "This isn't just a toy. It's a *collectible* toy. It's for collecting—not playing."

Patrick was still confused. "But then what do you do with it?"

"Lock it in a closet," explained SpongeBob. "Or maybe, on special occasions, display it on a shelf."

Patrick stared at the Bubble Blower. "Can I put it on *my* shelf, SpongeBob?" he asked.

"Patrick," said SpongeBob, "you don't have a shelf."

"I could *build* one," said Patrick. "Then I could look at the Blubble Bower—"

"Bubble Blower," corrected SpongeBob.

"—as I fall asleep," continued Patrick. "Please?" he pleaded. "Just for one night? I'll be your best friend."

"You already *are* my best friend," said SpongeBob. Then SpongeBob thought hard. He decided that best friends share all their things—even their favorite things. "All right, you can borrow the Bubble Blower for one night," he said.

"Hooray!" yelled Patrick as he grabbed the package and ran off. SpongeBob shouted after him, "Remember—don't open it!"

At nighttime SpongeBob got ready for bed. "Good night, Gary!" he said. "I sure am glad I let Patrick borrow my new Bubble Blower. That's what best friends do."

"Meow," said Gary.

"I'm sure he'll be extra careful with it," said SpongeBob. He patted Gary and climbed into bed.

But as he lay in bed SpongeBob started to worry about all the things Patrick might be doing with the Bubble Blower. Had he taken it out of the package? Was he using up all the soap bubbles? Or was he doing something really terrible, like breaking the Mermaid Man bubble wand?

FIGHT
EVIL
WITH
FIBER!

SpongeBob couldn't take it anymore. He got up, put on his clothes, and went downstairs. Gary followed him.

"Sorry, Gary," SpongeBob said. "I'm not taking you for a walk. I'm just going to sneak over to Patrick's house and make sure everything's okay with my new Bubble Blower."

Gary frowned.

"And don't give me that look," said SpongeBob.

SpongeBob creeped past Squidward's house. As he tiptoed up to Patrick's rock he thought about his precious Bubble Blower. "Please be in the box. . . . Please be in the box. . . . Please be in the box," he thought aloud.

SpongeBob entered Patrick's house as quietly as he could. Patrick was asleep and snoring loudly.

SpongeBob spotted the Bubble Blower on Patrick's new shelf. It was fine! Patrick hadn't broken it! He hadn't even opened it!

"I should have trusted him," said SpongeBob.

BUBBLE BLOWER

"See you in the morning, pal," whispered SpongeBob very quietly. But as he turned to go he tripped over a shell and fell with a loud crash!

Patrick sat up in bed, wide awake. "SpongeBob!" he yelled. "What are you doing here?"

"I'm sorry, Patrick," said SpongeBob, embarrassed. "I was just . . . um . . . well, I guess I was just a teensy bit worried about my Mermaid Man and Barnacle Boy Bubble Blower."

Patrick quickly put on his shorts. He was shocked. "You mean you didn't trust me? Your *best friend*? That's terrible! I can't believe it!"

Patrick was so upset that he started waving his arms and jumping up and down. He started knocking things over, sending his things crashing to the ground.

"My own best friend! Not trusting me!" he yelled. "I would never, ever break anything of yours! What do you think I am—careless?"

"Patrick, please!" called SpongeBob. "You're breaking all your stuff!"

Patrick stopped and looked around at all the things he'd broken. "Gee, SpongeBob. I guess I *am* a little bit careless," he said. "You were right to be worried. You'd better take your Bubble Blower home before I break it."

Patrick walked over toward the Bubble Blower, tripped, and almost knocked it off the shelf! "*You* pick it up!" he cried. "I shouldn't even touch it! I'm just a big, clumsy oaf!"

SpongeBob picked up the Bubble Blower and started to walk out of the house.
But then he stopped and turned around.
"Come on, Patrick!" he yelled. "Follow me!"
Patrick quickly followed.

Outside, SpongeBob began to take the packaging off the Bubble Blower.

"SpongeBob!" yelled Patrick. "What are you doing?"

"What good is a Bubble Blower if you can't blow bubbles with it?" asked SpongeBob. "Wanna play with it?"

"I sure do!" said Patrick.

SpongeBob dipped the wand into the bubble liquid and handed it to Patrick. "Here, Patrick," he said. "You can blow the first bubble."

"Wow," said Patrick, as his eyes widened. "The first blubble . . . I mean, bubble."

Patrick blew a big bubble, and then SpongeBob blew one, and they continued to blow bubbles into the wee hours of the morning.

Squidward didn't get much sleep that night.

SpongeBob's Secret Valentine

by David Lewman

illustrated by Heather Martinez

"Ready, Gary?" asked SpongeBob. His pet snail looked up and blinked. "Okay . . . fetch!" yelled SpongeBob as he lobbed a ball of kelp over Gary's head.

"Meow," said Gary, watching it fly by.

"Good effort, Gary!" said SpongeBob enthusiastically.

Sandy walked up with the kelp ball splattered all over her helmet. "Howdy, SpongeBob! Is this yours?"

"It sure is, Sandy!" he said. "Wanna play fetch with Gary and me?"

Sandy scraped the blob off her helmet and tossed it to him. "Sorry, SpongeBob, but I have to get home and make a special valentine for tomorrow. Adios!"

"Did you hear that, Gary?" asked SpongeBob. "I bet that special valentine Sandy's making is for me. I'd better start making one for her!"

"You like Sandy!" bellowed Patrick, who had crept up behind SpongeBob, startling him.

"Of course I like Sandy, Patrick. She's my friend."

"No, I mean you *really* like her," said Patrick. "If a boy gives a girl a valentine, it's a *really huge deal!*"

SpongeBob looked puzzled. "What do you mean?"

"Now you'll have to spend all your time with Sandy and you won't have time for any of your friends," explained Patrick. "Oh, SpongeBob, I'll miss you, little buddy!" With that, he ran off crying.

"Patrick, wait! Come back!" SpongeBob turned to Gary and shrugged. "You know, Gary, it's hard to believe, but I think Patrick might be wrong. On the other hand, I really don't want to lose any friends."

SpongeBob thought hard. Then he snapped his fingers. "I know! I'll ask Squidward!"

SpongeBob knocked on Squidward's door. "Squidward! Open up! It's an emergency!"

Squidward opened the door in a panic, dripping wet from his bath. "What? What's the emergency?" he asked, panting.

"Squidward, do you think I should give Sandy a valentine tomorrow?" Squidward just stared at SpongeBob. Then he slammed the door. "Hmm, Squidward seems busy," said SpongeBob. "Maybe I'll ask Mr. Krabs."

At the Krusty Krab, Mr. Krabs leaned back in his chair. "Sure, SpongeBob, I'd be glad to give you some advice. Save every penny you make—"

SpongeBob interrupted him. "I don't need advice about money, Mr. Krabs. I need advice about a girl."

Mr. Krabs leaped up and yelled, "Stay away from me only daughter, SpongeBob!"

SpongeBob looked confused. "I'm not talking about Pearl, Mr. Krabs. I'm talking about Sandy."

"Oh," said Mr. Krabs, wiping his brow. "That's a relief. What seems to be the problem?"

SpongeBob explained the whole valentine situation.

"Hmm," replied Mr. Krabs, scratching his chin. "As she is a land creature, there's really no telling what Sandy will think of your valentine. I suggest you go over to her treedome."

SpongeBob brightened up. "To ask her?"

"No!" answered Mr. Krabs. "To *spy* on her."

SpongeBob disguised himself as a piece of coral and sneaked up to Sandy's treedome.

Then, very quietly, he pressed his face against the glass. He looked all around but didn't see Sandy anywhere. "Oh, tartar sauce!" said SpongeBob. "She must be inside her treehouse. I've got to go in."

SpongeBob opened and closed the door to the dome as quietly as he could and shimmied up the tree. He peeked through the window and saw Sandy making a huge, red valentine.

Suddenly, her nose twitched. "I smell saltwater," she said. "Either my dome's sprung a leak, or there's an . . . INTRUDER!"

SpongeBob scrambled down the side of the tree and out of the dome as fast as he could. He could hear Sandy behind him yelling, "You'll never get away, ya thievin' varmint!" But he did get away—just barely.

SpongeBob slammed the front door behind him and leaned up against it, breathing hard. "I've got to get to work," he told Gary. "Sandy's making me the biggest valentine I've ever seen! I don't care what Patrick says—I'm going to make one for her!"

SpongeBob dove into his closet and came out with his arms full of materials. Then he flew into action: drawing, cutting, and pasting until the sun came up over Bikini Bottom.

"I'M READY!" he shouted at last, holding up a big, beautiful valentine with Sandy's name on it.

SpongeBob ran over to Sandy's place with the valentine. Just as he reached her treedome, Sandy came out carrying her huge valentine.

"Hey, Sandy!" said SpongeBob, grinning. "That's quite a valentine you've got there. It must be for somebody pretty special."

Sandy nodded. "Yup, it sure is, SpongeBob. My mother's a very special lady!"

"M-m-mother?" said SpongeBob, stammering. "That's great, Sandy."
He tried to keep his big, fancy valentine hidden behind his back.
"Who's that valentine for, SpongeBob?" asked Sandy.
SpongeBob shifted his feet uneasily. "Um, what valentine?"
"The one that has 'Sandy' on it," she said.

Blushing, SpongeBob handed her the valentine. "It's for you, Sandy, but it doesn't really mean anything, like that I won't get to see Patrick anymore or . . ."

"Gosh, SpongeBob!" said Sandy, smiling. "This valentine's purtier than a Texas barbecue on the Fourth of July!"
Sandy held the valentine up, admiring it. Then she frowned. "You know what this means, SpongeBob?"

SpongeBob looked nervous. "No, Sandy," he said. "What does it mean?"
"It means I've got to thank you by challenging you to a karate match!"

Wow, thought SpongeBob, my friendship with Sandy hasn't changed a bit. Patrick was wrong!

"HEEEYAH!" yelled Sandy, flying through the air.

"HEEEYAH!" screamed SpongeBob.

And they spent the rest of Valentine's Day happily chopping away at each other.

TO: SANDY

TO MOM

And the Winner Is . . .

by Jenny Miglis
illustrated by Caleb Meurer
Based on the teleplay *Big Pink Loser*
by Jay Lender, William Reiss, and Merriwether Williams

One morning Patrick received a package in the mail. It was a trophy! He could barely contain his excitement. "My very first award!" he cried with glee. "I've got to show SpongeBob!"

Patrick barreled through SpongeBob's front door. He cleared his throat and read aloud, "'For Outstanding Achievement in Achievement . . . SpongeBob SquarePants?' Huh? That's a funny way to spell my name!"

SpongeBob looked down at his feet. "Uh, Patrick, there must be some mistake," he said. "That award is for me."

"B-b-but I never won an award before," Patrick whined. "It's so shiny."
"I've got something else that's shiny in my coat closet! A button!"
said SpongeBob. "You can have it!"

"Goody! I'll get it!" Patrick cried. He flung open the door of a nearby closet. Awards and trophies of all shapes and sizes tumbled out.

"Not there!" SpongeBob cried. "That's my . . . award closet," he mumbled.

CRASH!

"Waah! I want an award!" Patrick wailed. "I'm not good at anything!"

SpongeBob wrapped his arm around Patrick's shoulder. "But you're Patrick STAR!" he exclaimed. "You can do anything you set your mind to!"

"Okay, I want to defeat the giant monkey men and save the ninth dimension!" Patrick said.

"That's too big. Something smaller," SpongeBob said.

"Defeat the little monkey men and save the eighth dimension?" Patrick asked.

SpongeBob sighed. "The smallest thing you can think of!" he said.

Patrick thought for a moment. "A job at the Krusty Krab?"

"Great idea!" said SpongeBob. "Let's go!"

"It was nice of Mr. Krabs to give me a job here. Do I get my award yet?" Patrick asked as he ate a Krabby Patty.

"You have to work for it," SpongeBob said, reminding him. "Pick up this order and take it to the customers," he instructed.

Patrick picked up the food and walked toward the table in the back. But just as he reached it he tripped, spilling Krabby Patties all over the floor.

"Good try," SpongeBob said. "But next time make sure the food actually gets to the customer."

"Why don't you answer the phone?" SpongeBob suggested.

"Aye, aye, captain!" Patrick exclaimed as the first call rang in.

"Is this the Krusty Krab?" the customer on the line asked.

"No, this is Patrick," Patrick replied and hung up.

The phone rang again. *Briiing! Briiing!*
"Hello, is this the Krusty Krab?" the second customer asked.

"NO! This is PATRICK!" Patrick hollered. "And I am NOT a crusty crab!" SpongeBob shook his head. "That's the name of the restaurant, Patrick." "Aww, fishpaste," Patrick said with a sigh. "I can't do anything right."

"Sure you can, Patrick," SpongeBob encouraged. "Uh, you can . . . you're good at . . . hmm . . ." He couldn't think of anything. "I've got it! I bet you know how to open a jar!"

SpongeBob took a jar of tartar sauce from the shelf and unscrewed the lid. "It's easy! Now you try. First, get a jar," he instructed.

Patrick rooted around in the refrigerator and emerged holding something that was clearly not a jar.

"No, Patrick, that's a pickle," SpongeBob said patiently.

After a few tries Patrick finally found a jar of jellyfish jelly.

"Good. Now just do exactly as I do. Exactly," said SpongeBob as he demonstrated.

"Exactly," Patrick repeated as he slowly turned the lid until it popped off.

"Oh, no! I broke it!" Patrick cried.

"No, Patrick, you did it!" SpongeBob exclaimed. "Good job!"

"I did?" Patrick asked with disbelief. "I opened the jar with my own hand! And it was all because you showed me how to do it, SpongeBob!"

"Patrick, if you do exactly what I do you'll have an award in no time!"

The next day Patrick greeted SpongeBob outside his house.

"Wow!" SpongeBob said. "It's amazing how a simple change of clothes can make a guy look just like . . . me!" He did a double take. "Huh?"

Patrick straightened his tie. "If I'm going to be a winner, I've got to dress like one," he declared.

"Okay, Patrick, whatever you say," SpongeBob said with a shrug. "Are you ready for work? I'm ready!"

"I'm ready! I'm ready! I'm ready!" Patrick chanted.

"Oops! Forgot my hat!" SpongeBob said.

"Oops! Me too!" Patrick said.

"Come on," SpongeBob said. "Back to the old grind."

"Come on, back to the old grind," Patrick repeated.

"Why are you copying me?" he asked Patrick.

"Why are you copying me?" Patrick repeated. "I want to win awards just like you, SpongeBob."

"Well, it's annoying, so stop it!" SpongeBob cried.

Patrick shrugged his shoulders. "Stop it," he mumbled under his breath.

"Aaaaaagh!" SpongeBob screamed. Then he had an idea. "Hi! My name is Patrick Star!" he said. "I'm the laziest, pinkest starfish in Bikini Bottom and I wish I were ME and not SpongeBob!"

But this time Patrick didn't imitate SpongeBob. "What's so great about being a big pink nobody? I was never closer to an award than the minute I started copying you," he said and hung his head.

Just then a delivery truck pulled up.
"Trophy delivery!" the truck driver called out.
"Must be another award for SpongeBob
TrophyPants!" Patrick sneered. "What's it for this
time, perfect squareness?"

SpongeBob took the trophy and held it up to the light. "'For Doing Absolutely Nothing Longer Than Anyone Else,'" he read, "'Patrick Star.'" SpongeBob couldn't believe his eyes. "Patrick! This trophy is for you!"

"For me?" Patrick gasped. "I always knew I'd win an award!"

"So, what are you going to do now that you've won it?" SpongeBob asked. Patrick propped himself up against the trophy. "Nothing, of course," Patrick said. "I've got to protect my title!"

SpongeBob SquarePants

SpongeBob and the Princess

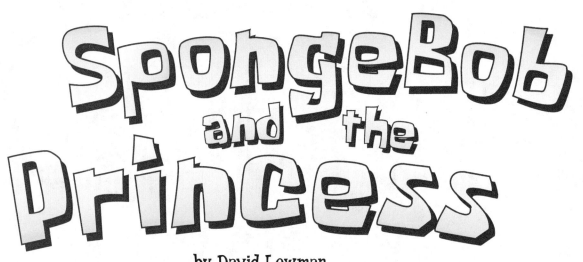

SpongeBob and the Princess

by David Lewman

illustrated by Clint Bond

At the Krusty Krab, SpongeBob was happily pushing a mop across the floor. *"I'm mopmopmoppin' that Krusty floor,"* he sang to himself.

"SpongeBob!" yelled Mr. Krabs. "I'm going to count me beautiful money," said Mr. Krabs. "So no visitors. Got that?"

"Aye, aye, Mr. Krabs," said SpongeBob, just as a loud truck pulled up outside. *Honk! Honk!*

"Welcome to the outside of the Krusty Krab. May I help you?" SpongeBob shouted to the driver, trying to make himself heard over the noise of the truck.

"Where's Mr. Krabs?" the driver asked.

"Counting his money, so he's not to be disturbed," answered SpongeBob. "Maybe I can help you."

"What?" yelled the driver.

SpongeBob cupped his hands to his mouth. "Maybe I can help you!"

"Tell Mr. Krabs that Princess Napkins will be here tomorrow," said the driver.

"What?" yelled SpongeBob.

"Princess delivery will be here tomorrow!" the driver shouted back.

"Got it!" said SpongeBob, giving a big thumbs-up. The driver drove off. "Hoppin' clams," said SpongeBob. "Wait till Squidward hears this!"

SpongeBob burst into the Krusty Krab. "Guess what,
Squidward! A princess'll be here tomorrow!"

Squidward didn't look up. "What princess would be caught dead in this dump?"
he asked gloomily. But then he brightened. "Unless it's . . . Princess Neptuna!
It doesn't seem likely, but for once, SpongeBob, I believe you! I *love* royalty!
They're so . . . *royal!*"

SpongeBob grinned. "I can't wait to tell Patrick and Sandy and Mrs. Puff and—"

Squidward shook his head. "No, no, don't tell anyone. Royal people love their privacy." Squidward figured he had a much better chance of getting Princess Neptuna's autograph if no one else was around.

"Really?" said SpongeBob, puzzled. "I thought princesses *loved* crowds."

Squidward sniffed. "You commoner. You know nothing about royalty."

SpongeBob thought hard. "Well, I *have* to tell Mr. Krabs."

"No!" yelled Squidward. "He'll ruin everything."

"But, Squidward," said SpongeBob, "it's my duty as a Krusty Krab employee!"

Squidward put his arm around SpongeBob. "Listen, SpongeBob," he said, "would you like me to teach you how to behave around royalty?"

SpongeBob's eyes grew big. "You'd teach me, Squidward?"

"Of course," said Squidward, smiling.

"Tonight?" asked SpongeBob, his eyes growing even bigger.

"Um, okay," said Squidward.

"At your house?" SpongeBob's eyes were huge. "With snacks?"

Squidward swallowed hard. "Sure, SpongeBob. I'm . . . inviting you . . . to my house . . . for royalty lessons and . . . snacks."

"HOORAY!" SpongeBob shouted. "I'll be there! And tomorrow the princess will be here!"

In his office Mr. Krabs heard SpongeBob shouting. "Better see what me employees are up to," he said, hurrying over to a picture on the wall. He lifted it and peered through a peephole just in time to hear SpongeBob say, "Tomorrow the princess will be here!"

"Princess?" whispered Mr. Krabs. "Princesses are rich! And people love to see 'em. People who could be MY PAYING CUSTOMERS! All I have to do is let everybody know a princess is coming to the Krusty Krab tomorrow! Hmm . . ."

That night Squidward tried to teach SpongeBob how to act properly around a princess. "No, no, SpongeBob," he scolded. "Never giggle when you bow to Princess Neptuna."

"But, Squidward," said SpongeBob. "I can't help it. Patrick looks kinda funny."

Patrick adjusted his crown. "Gee, thanks a lot, SpongeBob," he said. "I think I look beautiful."

Meanwhile Mr. Krabs was busy putting up signs all over Bikini Bottom announcing Princess Neptuna's arrival at the Krusty Krab. He chuckled to himself. "This ought to bring in the customers," he said. "*And their money!*"

PRINCESS NEPTUNA WANTS YOU

Krusty Krab

BUS

MEET THE PRINCESS TOMORROW ONLY!

MEET THE PRINCESS TOMORROW ONLY!

MEET THE PRINCESS TOMORROW ONLY!

MEET THE PRINCESS TOMORROW ONLY!

As SpongeBob approached the Krusty Krab the next morning, he saw almost all of Bikini Bottom waiting outside. "Gee," he said, "there sure are a lot of people hungry for delicious Krabby Patties today."

Just then Squidward showed up. "Oh, no!" he cried. "They must all be here to see Princess Neptuna!"

He angrily turned to SpongeBob. "You blabbed to everyone about the princess!"

"No, Squidward," answered SpongeBob. "I was over at your house, remember?"

Squidward scrunched up his face in confusion. "Then how did they all find out?"

"RIGHT THIS WAY!" barked Mr. Krabs. "THIS WAY TO SEE THE PRINCESS! CUSTOMERS WITH MONEY ONLY!"

The truck from the day before pulled up. An eager SpongeBob ran over, "When will the princess be here?" he whispered.

The driver scratched his head and gave SpongeBob a blank look.

"Yesterday you told me to tell Mr. Krabs, 'A princess will be here tomorrow,'" explained SpongeBob.

The driver stared at SpongeBob and then started laughing. "I said, 'The Princess delivery will be here tomorrow.' Y'know, Princess Napkins."

SpongeBob's mouth dropped open. "You mean Princess Neptuna isn't coming?"

"Nope," the driver replied, unloading several boxes onto the ground. "But here are your napkins. See ya!"

SpongeBob stared at the boxes. "What good are napkins when I promised everyone a princess?" he thought aloud.

SpongeBob spotted Patrick walking by. "Patrick!" he said.
"Am I glad to see you! I need you to dress up as the
princess again to fool that big crowd of customers!"

Patrick shook his head. "No way, SpongeBob.
Last night you said I looked funny."

"Yeah, but . . . but," said SpongeBob, sputtering.

"No buts about it," said Patrick stubbornly. "I'm not going to look ridiculous in front of all those people." And he put on his beanie propeller hat and turned to walk away.

"But, Patrick," SpongeBob begged, "who am I going to get to be the princess?"

"Hello, loyal subjects from Bikini Bottom!" SpongeBob called to the crowd. "I am your princess!"

Everyone turned and stared at SpongeBob. "That's Princess Neptuna?" someone shouted.

"Of course I am!" squeaked SpongeBob. "Well, it's sure been great to see you. And now if you'll excuse me . . ."

"THAT'S NOT PRINCESS NEPTUNA!" said a guy with a very loud voice. "THAT'S JUST SOME GUY DRESSED UP IN A PRINCESS COSTUME!"

The crowd murmured angrily.

"GET HIM!" they yelled. Everyone started to rush toward SpongeBob!

Before the crowd reached SpongeBob, a magnificent boat pulled up. The door opened, and a princess climbed out. "Hello, everyone," she said, smiling and waving. "I'm Princess Neptuna."

SpongeBob hoped he could remember the royalty lessons Squidward had given him. He bowed several times and got down on one knee. Taking her hand in his, SpongeBob said, "Hello, Princess Neptuna, what brings you to our humble establishment, the Krusty Krab?"

"Well," she answered, "I saw the crowd, so I stopped to see what was going on. I just *love* crowds!"

THE
KRUSTY
KRAB

Princess Neptuna signed autographs for everyone—including Squidward. She even tried a Krabby Patty. "This Krabby Patty is a delicious morsel, SpongeBob," she said. "But it's a little messy."

SpongeBob brought over a box. "How would you like your very own box of Princess Napkins?" he asked.

The princess smiled. "You sure know how to treat a princess, SpongeBob!"

Bottoms Up!

Jokes From Bikini Bottom

by David Lewman
illustrated by Caleb Meurer

Are you ready for some nautical nonsense?

Knock, knock.

Who's there?

Me.

Me who?

Meow.

(It must be Gary!)

How does SpongeBob begin
bedtime stories for his pet snail, Gary?
"Once upon a slime . . ."

He wanted to get it off his chest.

Why did SpongeBob
move his alarm clock
onto a barrel?

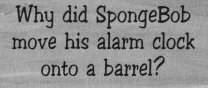

What snack goes best with an underwater lunch?

Splurt!

zzle!

A bag of potato drips.

potato Drips

What position would Mr. Krabs play if he were on a baseball team?

Pinch hitter.

Why did SpongeBob and Patrick climb onto the fishermens' lines?

They were playing hooky.

Bzzz

Why did Patrick bring nose plugs to go jellyfishing?

He thought they were going smellyfishing.

BZzz

BZzz

Why did SpongeBob
bring musical
instruments to
Jellyfish Fields?

*Because jellyfish
love to jam!*

SHUCK!

Jive!

What is Sandy's favorite carnival ride?

The Tilt-a-Squirrel.

What does Sandy call two trees floating in the ocean? *Swimming trunks.*

What does Sandy like to do on her computer?

Surf the Internut.

zzzzzzzzzzzzzzzz . . .

152

Why did Pearl get all dressed up to go to the Goo Lagoon?

She heard there was a beach ball.

What does Plankton surf on?

Microwaves

So cool!

Why did Squidward buy this house?

Why did Squidward squirt ink at SpongeBob?

He was just squidding around.

He wanted to get a head.

Honk!

Squawk!

What happened when
SpongeBob karate-chopped
Squidward?

He flipped his squid.

giggle
giggle

Knock, knock.
  Who's there?
Toodle.
  Toodle who?

You're leaving
so soon?

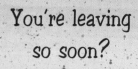